MARLEY O'CONNOR

Eternal Descent

Dedication

This book I am dedicating to my best friend Kelsey who has hyped me since she has known me. She has been there supporting and believing in me since day one. This one is for you, BatKelz. I love you!

Forward

Please be advised that this book does have some sexual content, some drug references, violence, and religious views, possibly not favored by all.

But if you are a mild smut soul with an addiction to misunderstood grey demonic characters, this book is for you.

Table of Contents

Prologue

Isaiah 14:22

~ 7 ~

"How you have fallen from heaven, morning star, son of dawn!"

But what if Lucifer found redemption through God's favorite
creation?

Chapter One

Lucifer

I no longer sit by God's side. I no longer float above with my brothers, walk the streets of gold, or see who arrives through the pearly gates. I haven't been to the heavens since I was sent crashing down, since Michael struck me into this dirt-filled domain.

Sometimes I crave the unity I had above, but following orders was never my strong suit. Now I sit on the outskirts of Scotland. I moved to many places in my immortal life. And Scotland became a final home, or as much of a home, as I could ever have.

I made a cottage away from the humans in Crovie, Aberdeenshire. Far back on the outskirts. It wasn't a large cabin. It was modest. Made of logs with a brick chimney and porch.

Life was peaceful. I watched humans go about their daily lives. They never knew the devil was on their home front. I would sometimes go down and observe them.

I would change a few things about my appearance. My eyes are now the fiery glow of embers and there is a long scar down the left side of my eye. I once held four faces and four wings, a cherub angel. But when I fell, my powerful aura was stripped half mass.

My four faces became one and my wings became one set and turned black. My toned body stayed, and my once long golden hair turned charcoal black. I stood tall, too tall for most humans. I towered over them.

Every day I would take my Earl Gray tea and stand outside my home, watching the sunrise. I had a horse whom I rescued a long time ago. He was white as a fresh snowfall, with the deepest blue eyes. I named him Noel.

I had fallen, but I still had power. I wasn't entirely weak. I gave Noel the power of eternity if he stayed by my side. And since that day, he would walk up to me and watch with me, as I sipped my morning tea.

That day was like any other. I rose early, made my tea, walked outside, and watched the sunrise with Noel.

But this time, something hit me like I had been shocked. I dropped my teacup and gripped my chest. I lost balance and dropped to my knees.

A scorching heat flooded my chest. I rolled in pain. Noel whined and nudged me with his nose. I softly touched his nose. The heat started calming, but that electrical shock pulled me in the direction of the town.

I tried to resist the pull and ignore the agitated pain, but I couldn't, it was too strong. I took a deep breath and stood.

"Stay, Noel. I will be back."

Noel snorted and watched me walk to town.

Chapter Two

Lucifer

I made it to the edge of town. I quickly turned my eyes to cyan blue and left my scar. People stared in wonder, and disgust, or didn't look at me.

I have an aura about me that scares them, another symptom of my curse. The pull directed me towards the coffee shop where I sometimes go to observe the humans.

It's a Sunday afternoon, so Old Brigid Café was crowded with churchgoers and college students. I stand a little to the corner of the door, observing as always. But this time with a mission.

In the back of the room, my eyes fell on a table. I glide my eyes over the people there. On the outside of the table is a guy with dark hair. His sides and back are shaved, except the long middle. He's wearing a checkered red and black flannel, dark jeans, and brown boots. He looks well-built.

But something is sparkling in the corner of my eyes. I move to who he's speaking to. And that is when a bright light hits my eyes. And the heat is back.

I squint and try to focus on this human. I was moving the light to surround her instead of engulfing her.

My heart skips and my pants become tight in my midsection. There is a girl in the corner. She sits on the booth, back against the corner wall.

She has long reddish-brown hair, that falls in waves. Her face is like a graceful flower petal, with delicate features and a slender, elegant shape.

I don't know how long I stared, but it must have been for a while because we locked our eyes. I take in her shimmering forest greens that trace me with curiosity.

My blood starts to run like fire in my veins, and the pull wants to drag me to her side. I have the urge to pin her down and make her mine. But the last woman I loved, turned into a demon.

She tilts her head at me, and I can feel her eyes running over me, examining me. I swallow hard and push the pull down. I jerk the door open and run back to my small cottage.

Chapter Three

Elizabeth

I feel him before I see him. I look behind Jaspir and we lock eyes. I feel as if something knocks into my heart. Heat licks my insides. I want to grip him and pull him into my soul.

I raised my back from the wall but watched him bolt out the door.

"E? What's up? Jaspir asks, turning around to look.

I break my hypnotic stare and bring my attention back to him. He shrugs his shoulders after finding no one there.

"Anyways, how is art class? Feel like I'm always catching a ball. You and Hawk are always doing something."

I smile at him. I've known them my whole life. I've known Thorn only a year longer than Jaspir. Jaspir came into our lives in first grade. He's a loud and outgoing soul, while Hawthorn and I are quiet. Thorn is the quietest of us three.

Jaspir goes on about his day, but my eyes look behind him, into the sky. I can feel this presence calling to my instincts.

Suddenly my break alarm goes off, causing me to jolt a little. Jaspir grabs my hand.

"What's is up, E? You seem on edge."

"It's nothing. I'm fine. Come on. The break is over. We gotta go."

I gather my things and we rush out of the café. Jaspir runs into his football teammates and takes off with them. I'm left standing on the sidewalk.

My eyes scan over the cliff. I see the top of a chimney, far back on the cliff. My body wants to run to it, but I shove that feeling down and walk to my last class.

Chapter Four

Lucifer

Once I arrived at my cabin, I hurriedly fed Noel and locked myself in my study. The girl's face ran through my mind on repeat. She wasn't afraid or disgusted of me. She was intrigued. Her eyes sparkled when she ran them over me. I wanted her, I wanted her so badly. But the last mortal I had pleasures with, went badly.

This was two hundred years ago. She was beautiful. Golden curls flowed over her slender shoulders. Her skin was soft and the perfect shade of chocolate. Her eyes were wide and deep with hazel coloring. She was stunning.

I wanted her too. And I got her. I fell in love with her. But like the others, I lost her too. I lost her more deeply than the others. My blood is like heroine. The humans who I would pick for slaves of sex, I would give my blood too.

Eventually, they would take too much and slowly die. Just like overdosing but at an agonizing pace. But my love, my love turned them into hell beings. To love me, was to lose your humanity.

I met her in London. She was middle class, and smart. She wasn't very keen on parties and had no friends. Her books were her friends. I was drawn to her enjoyment of solitude. I felt as though I had someone who knew true loneliness.

So, one day, as I watched her from afar, she called to me. She turned from her book, on her favorite bench.

"Well, come out. Or are you going to hide some more?" She smiled.

I approached her with caution. She placed her book on her lap and tapped beside her. I hesitated, but she tapped beside her again. I slowly took the seat. She turned towards me.

"Why do you watch me? I've felt your eyes for a while now, sir."

I took in her deep dimples and her slender shoulders. Her golden curls brushed against them. My hands itched to do the same.

"I find you interesting."

"Hmmm…well what are you interested in?"

I watched as she moved closer to me. I raised my hand and tapped her forehead.

"This." I smiled

"My head? How odd." She laughed

"I've seen you for a while now. You don't like parties. You don't like people much. You like those." I pointed at her books

She stared at me for a minute, then stood and took my hand. From that point for years, we spent every waking moment together. Until one day, I felt my love finally break free.

We made love, and the next morning, I found her in the bathroom. The woman I fell in love with, wasn't there. Her body was, but her soul was gone.

She faced me, and her eyes were now like coal, and dripping sable-colored oil.

"Alice? What? How? I don't see your soul."

I watched as an evil grin spread against her face. Her white teeth were now jagged, and a forked tongue licked her lips.

"My dear Lu, you did this. That little love of yours. It changed me."

I stepped to her and held her hands. My heart was breaking. I couldn't believe my love and the act of my love took her soul.

"I'm so sorry, Alice. Let me fix this. Please. Let me help you."

She ripped herself out of my arms and walked around me.

"Help me? Fix me? No. You made me stronger, Lucifer. With me like this, one day we can rule this rock and all its weak humans. Plus, I like this new me. Don't you?"

She stared at me. That evil grin is still there. My Alice was gone, and I was the reason.

"You aren't my Alice anymore. You are just her body. You are a demon now."

She laughed loudly and pranced around me.

"Alice is gone. A new Alice is here. Because of you. Too bad you don't like her. But I'm keeping her."

And before I could stop her, she punched me in the temple, and I collapsed. She knew my strength wasn't that of my formal self.

I lay on the floor, falling into the dark. I felt her come by my ear and lick me.

"Goodbye, Lu."

And that was the last of her I've ever seen again. I look at the news for any weird happenings, but never anything. Noel's whining broke my memories, and I realized the evening had broken through.

So, I removed myself from my study and headed outside. I fed him and watched the little town below. The pull is still there, but it isn't as intense as earlier. I wanted her. Her light, her soul calls to me and I want to grip it in my hands. I wanted to feel every inch of her.

But I fought it down. I don't want to turn her into Alice. I turn from the town to Noel. I pat his head and kiss his snout before ushering him into his barn.

"Goodnight, my Noel. Sleep tight."

I shut the door and walked to my cottage's door. I turned the knob slowly and sighed. I change and lay in bed. I force myself to sleep.

Chapter Five

Elizabeth

Art class passed quickly, but my mind was full of that guy's face, and I couldn't help but sketch it. I stared down at it, running my finger across his scar. Even his picture sends this yearning emotion through me.

"Hey Ell. Who's that?"

I looked up to find Thorn staring at my picture. His gray eyes trace all the details in my picture. I shut it quickly and turned towards him.

"Oh, no one I know. I saw him enter the pub earlier, and thought he seemed mysterious and well kind of drew him." I smile awkwardly.

Thorn stared at me, trying to read me. He was always like that. Very calm, and observant. He never really lets loose unless he's alone with Jaspir.

"Huh, okay. Well, what are your plans for the rest of the night then?"

"I'm not sure. I have a painting I need to finish for this class.

The end of the first semester is this week, and it's a big grade point. You?"

Thorn intertwined his arm with mine and started walking us from the college towards my apartment.

"Well, I have to finish a software thing for my gaming content course and then help our puppy finish his end-of-semester project."

"Awe, what would he do without you?" I smile

"Well, he wouldn't make it anywhere. That football playing has messed that brain of his up."

I giggle and stop in front of my apartment door. It's so close to the college that it only takes a short while to get there.

"Don't stay up too late, El"

Thorn kisses my cheek, and I watch as he runs down the sidewalk, back to college to find Jaspir.

I unlock my door and head in. My apartment isn't anything flashy. It's a one-bedroom loft. The walls are a soft eggshell white and my carpet is fluffy and black.

I was never sure why they chose black. I have a small kitchen. My queen-sized day bed is shoved in the far back corner of the room.

My old white secretary's desk is in front of my bay window. And my very worn easel is placed in the center.

I place my bag and coat on my desk chair and stare out my window. The evening had turned into night, and I felt drained by the sun.

I changed into my oversized tee shirt, turned on some music, and drifted into blissful sleep.

Chapter Six

Lucifer

The sun shone through my window, waking me. I stretched and started my normal morning routine. But something ached in me.

That pull was back. I tried shaking it away. But it was still there. Like an itch that didn't go away with a scratch.

I hopped in the shower. I placed my hands on the wall and bent my head down. I closed my eyes and felt the steaming hot water trace every inch of my body. Her face came flying into my mind. The way her eyes tracked my body.

The hunger I felt when our eyes locked. I became hard, and I couldn't hold it back any longer. I gripped my cock, and thrust into my hand, quick and hard to the image of her face.

The release came fast and sweetly. I heaved heavily and slammed my hand into the wall. I stared at the dent, knowing that was as close to having her as I would be able to.

I dressed and went to see Noel. He slept in late today, so I left his breakfast and started into the little town.

I breathed in the crisp air and drank my tea. I needed to go down there, that pull was just too much for me to ignore it.

So, I went in and threw on my long black wool trench coat over my maroon suit. I braided my long hair loosely turned my collar up and headed out my door.

Chapter Seven

Elizabeth

My alarm blared in my ears. I slammed my hand on top of the clock and sighed. The sun broke through my sheer curtains, brightening the whole apartment.

I stretched and checked my phone. Hawthorn texted and wanted me to meet him and Jaspir at the cafe.

I tossed the phone to the side and looked through my closet. The cafe was only a few doors down, so I took a moment.

I chose a pair of black skinny jeans, a long knitted black sweater with white daises, and maroon combat boots. I combed my hair and left it down, placing a maroon beanie on it.

I took one last look at myself and grimaced. All I saw was my father. I hated that. I didn't want to look like the man who beat my mother, my brother, and me. I felt my phone buzz, breaking me from my dark thoughts.

"Shit," I spoke out loud.

Thorn messaged again, so I took off. I ran down the street to meet them.

I pushed through the door and watched as they waved me over.

I dropped my bag and took a seat in a black cloth recliner.

"So how did last night go?" I asked

"Jay decided not to study which meant, I couldn't either."

"Awe, so no one got to their projects then?" I giggled.

"Nope. What did you do then, E?" Jaspir asked

"Nothing but sleep, and it was the best I've gotten in a long time."

Hawthorn rose and went to get our drinks.

"So E, who's this guy you drew?"

I stared at him, and then back at Hawthorn who juggled our drinks.

"No one. I don't know who he is. I saw him the other day and wanted to draw him. But it's no big deal. So don't worry. Either of you." I stared directly at Thorn.

He hands me my toasted vanilla latte and smirks.

"Hey, you only talk to us. So, if I see you drawing some random dude in your book, I have questions and have to pass it to Jay here."

I roll my eyes and sit my drink down.

"Well, aren't we supposed to be studying?" I smirk

"Ugh. Why did I choose college?" Jay complains

"Well, what else are you gonna do with that football scholarship? Can't just play ball dumbass." Thorn laughs.

I started to pull my sketchbook out and that's when I felt him.

The burning sensation trailing my nerve endings, and the desire to be consumed by his lips go wild inside me.

Then I heard the bell of the cafe door open and knew he was there.

"El, you, okay?"

I look up at Thorn and smile.

"Yes, I'm fine. Let's work."

Chapter Eight

Lucifer

I made it to the coffee shop and stood a little off to the side, staring. That pull was stronger now. I sighed and gave in.

I walked into the shop. I ordered and found a small table in the back, where I could see the door. My coffee arrived at my table with a newspaper. I sipped on my coffee and read the paper.

I knew she was there before even seeing her. I felt her soul. It shouted at me. Electrical shocks pinched at my body. I looked from the newspaper to her.

She was at the far back on the other side of the shop, with two guys opposite her on a loveseat. The guy I saw yesterday with Viking-style hair and flannel.

But the other guy was new. He was her height, shorter than the other man.

He had long brown hair that was pulled in a ponytail. He wore a faded blue jean jacket, a black plain shirt, blue jeans, and harness boots.

He seemed quieter compared to other man. I watched as she laughed with them and occasionally playfully smacked their shoulders.

A jealous spark ran through me, and

I glared at the two men. I watched them from my newspaper for a while before I headed to the bathroom.

I splashed my face with water and paced my breathing before going back to my table. The two men rose and kissed her on each cheek before leaving her.

She sat alone now, staring at an open notebook. She chewed on her pencil top. I watched as she stared at her notebook, unfocused.

Every move she made; I watched her body. The heat was exploding in my groin, and my hunger started tearing at my stomach. I knew I had to go. I rose and took off out the door.

Chapter Nine

Elizabeth

I felt him get up and leave. I couldn't just sit and ignore this impulse to be around him. I shoved my books into my bag and ran out.

He was standing off to the opening of an alleyway beside the cafe, staring up at the stars. I approached him. He seemed a bit startled to see me smiling up at him.

"Hi there."

He turned to face me. His eyes scanned my body.

The deep blue took all of me in.

"Oh, hi. I don't think we've met." he smiled

"No, not at all. But do you make it a habit to stare all evening at girls, and their friends?" I smirked.

"Ummm…I'm not sure what you mean?" he acted confused

"Well, maybe it was just my eyes playing tricks then. But even so, I'll be here tomorrow with Jaspir and Hawthorn, if you'd like to say hello or hang around for a bit."

Before he could reply, I stood up on my tiptoes and placed a kiss on his cheek. I moved away, did a little wave, and took off to my apartment. My body wanted so much more, but I had to go. I felt this overwhelming desire to jump him.

I made it to my apartment and threw my bag on the floor. I changed into my pajamas, and slowly ran my hand into my shorts. I stroked my clit to his face and voice.

I rubbed with one finger and used my other fingers to drive in and out of my vagina. I went fast, and I felt it all rush. I came with such force that I instantly felt drained.

I wiped my hands off and fell asleep.

Chapter Ten

<u>Lucifer</u>

She stood up on her tiptoes and placed a kiss on my cheek. I stood there staring at her in awe. She wasn't afraid of me; she wasn't disgusted by me.

All I smelled of her was curiosity and maybe a hint of desire. I placed my hand over where she held her lips, and a small tremor ran down my spine. I had never craved someone as much as her. Not even Alice.

I shook off my nerves and slowly walked down the sidewalk, towards the water. Noel was cozy in his barn, and my body craved the cold air. I made it to a small bench placed on the beach.

It was old and worn. But it was placed in the perfect spot. The water would come up, and tickle just the tips of your toes. I took off my loafers, and dress socks, sitting them beside me. I watched as the waves came up, and the remaining wave would lightly kiss my toes.

I smiled to myself. The night was clear, and the stars were bright. I breathed in a deep amount of crisp air and sighed. I knew what was beyond those stars. The wonders and kinship.

Tonight was lonelier than normal. I stared into the sky, peace washing over my body. I closed my eyes, sinking deeper into the cold breeze, and the sounds of the water.

"Lucifer, be careful. They will take your light."

I jumped up, looking for the voice that spoke in my ear. It seemed so familiar. But I know none of my fellow angels would dare speak to me, let alone warn me of danger.

I'm turning and looking all around. But no one was there. There are no feathers on the ground, no large footsteps in the sand.

There is only me and the waves. I rub my hands through my hair and shake my head.

I felt tired, and the peace was gone by whoever it was that warned me. But the warning wasn't correct. My light was stolen a long time ago. All I have now is dying embers.

Embers that barely have fire. I dust my feet and put on my shoes. As I head home, I feel like someone is watching me but I never see anyone.

My little cottage is like a welcome sign as I approach it. The warmth of having a home embraces me each time I come back. I hear Noel demand his dinner as he hears me arrive. I laugh to myself. I always manage to find myself being close to the ones with the most attitude. Maybe that's why Michael and I always butted heads.

As I give Noel his dinner, my heart becomes heavy. There are clear beautiful nights like tonight that never give me complete peace.

They only tease me with a few moments of it, and then that is when it hits me. I have only Noel to share beautiful nights with. My family has disowned me, and the humans fear me.

Father's curse intended for me to have a long lonesome eternity. I would never be like Hades. Even he has managed to find a soul to love him.

I tuck Noel into her barn and head back into my home. I put on some tea, and light the fireplace in the living room.

Each room of my cottage has a bookcase in it. The living room isn't large. It's just right. There is a small loveseat under the window on the right side.

The fireplace is set into the wall facing the island of the kitchen. And to the left side is my tall oak bookcase with a recliner beside it. A small end table rests at the end of the loveseat and recliner.

I grabbed my tea and sat in the recliner. I watch the fire bounce and dance. It's mesmerizing. My light used to be as well. I would do tricks with it for the other angels, even some of the souls that arrived through the gates.

My blonde hair would glow, and my bright blue eyes were a light of their own.

I was something God was very proud of. I was his favorite son. I was the seal of perfection. I was an angel of great wisdom and beauty.

I was also young. Me and the others were created before the universe, before mankind.

We witnessed the birth of the world. As time went on, and the more I realized how perfect he had made me, I wanted to sit above him.

I wanted to rule. That was my downfall. Pride gripped my heart. I took a third of the angels and went to war with heaven and the angels who were still loyal to God.

And at the end, Michael was the one to bring me and my loyal angels down.

The Bible and the preachers say other angels came with me. They did, but they didn't stay beside me. They went and did heinous things upon God's creation. Most of them have died now. They weren't so lucky to have immortality once they got here like me.

I am on the earth alone. No one in heaven or earth beside me. I look up out the window and watch the sky until my eyes feel heavy, and I fall asleep

Chapter Eleven

I wake up before my alarm sounds. My insides are going crazy. Today I saw him. At least I'll have my guys if I feel overwhelmed. But a part of me knows I'm okay in his presence. As if that's where I belong.

I strode to the bathroom for a hot shower. I let the water warm my bones and blush my skin. I step out and dry myself off. The weather is cool, but I slip into a tight gray sweater dress with some fleece line tights, and my worn maroon boots.

I combed my wavy hair and put on mascara. Once again, I stare at the mirror, hating myself. My dad left when I was fifteen.

He abused us since I could walk. He was a drunk monster who hated his children and wife. He pushed us so far. He left us but he only left me alive, and somewhat intact. I survived his hands. But at what cost?

I shook the thoughts from my mind. I grabbed my art book and supplies and headed towards the shop.

Chapter Twelve

Lucifer

My body feels sore as my eyes open. I fell asleep in my recliner.

I even I, an immortal can become sore from uncomfortable seating. I stretch my body out and look around. I can hear Noel whining about his morning routine. I look at my grandfather's clock by the door.

I overslept. My mind took a while to turn off last night. I skipped my tea and dress. I slip on some blue jeans in my favorite bootcut trim, my favorite loose thick dark forest green sweater, and black dress boots.

I make my way out to Noel. He glares at me with a large sigh, and I laugh.

"Now, Noel, I slept in a little later today. I am sorry, my friend." I smile

He walks over with a sass to the gallop of his hooves and puts his head in my hands.

"Awe. That's a good boy, Noel. Now eat. I have a business to attend to today."

Noel snorts and goes about his way. I watch him for a moment before I make my way back into the cottage.

I grab a book I've been meaning to read and slip into my beige dress trench coat. I went down the hill to the coffee shop.

Chapter Thirteen

Elizabeth

I saw Hawthorn and Jaspir had already made it and I rushed over.

"Hey guys! Did you read my text about a new person joining us?"

"You mean the guy in your sketchbook? Thorn says.

I blush and take a seat between them.

"Yes, that guy."

Jaspir turns to Thorn and me and folds his arms across his chest.

"Why? Why do you need to get to know this guy? Be friends with him?"

I stared off, trying to figure out the answer. But I don't know why. I just feel this draw, this pull towards him. I need to fill it; I need to be around him. As if that's where I belong.

"No matter. Maybe our little El is trying to be more social."

Thorn answers for me

"Really? E be social? Since when? And why is it with a guy who seems like bad news?" He scoffs.

"Whatever her reason, is her reason," Thorn says with what seems like some kind of unknown knowledge to me.

I shake off his odd reply and bring out my sketchbook.

"Have you guys done any work on your projects yet? You know they are due Sunday."

Jaspir wraps his arm around my shoulders and playfully side hugs me.

"You know me. I'm more of a last-minute guy." He smiles

I roll my eyes and look at Thorn.

"What about you, Thorn?"

But he doesn't look at me. He looks at the door.

"Looks like your new friend showed."

I look at him and instantly become consumed with need.

Chapter Fourteen

Lucifer

I arrive around Noon. I looked around and spotted her with the two guys from before.

Before I even move, I feel her turn around and smile at me.

My heart starts hammering inside my chest. It's like she felt my presence. I watch as she tells her friends to wait and skips slightly over to me.

She grins up at me and offers her hand.

"I see you made it. We never exchanged names last night. I'm Elizabeth. And you?"

"I'm Lucifer."

She is taken aback a little and stares at me for a second. I stand there, embarrassment building deep in my stomach. And then I watch as she smiles.

"Hmmm…. That's the first time I've heard that. Outside of the bible of course."

"My father was a religious man." I awkwardly smile.

She smiles again and grabs my hand. I feel like I just touched an outlet with silver. But it doesn't hurt. It awakens me.

I feel like fainting. I can see the sparkling light around her. But she doesn't notice my reaction because she's dragging me towards her friends.

"Come On, Lu. I'll introduce you to my guys."

She drags me over to her friends. She plops down on a loveseat between the two men.

The Viking one is glaring at me and the other is just taking me in. I slowly sit across from them in a recliner.

"We haven't ordered yet. What would you like?" She smiled at me

"Ummm, black coffee is fine. Thank you." I nodded

"I called that, Thorn. You owe me five dollars." She smirks

I watch as she bounces away to order everyone's coffee. I feel their eyes on me, so I turn to face them. I see them better now since we are so close.

The Viking looking one is at least six feet tall, but I'm still taller. He's of a lean build. He's wearing a gray loose tee shirt, dark gray sweatpants, and black Converse. His hair is tied in a man bun.

I look over at the other one. This one is quiet. Everything about him is quiet. Unlike the other man who I could feel a thunderstorm off, I can't feel any kind of rage. He's like the calm before the storm. He watches me like a cat.

He also has changed his look a bit except he has left the hat and vest off. But he wears a dark blue tee shirt, loose worn jeans, and boots. His long black hair hangs loose down his back.

He's Elizabeth's height and more of a brawny build. He doesn't glare at me like the other one does. It's as if he is analyzing me.

Elizabeth comes back with the coffees, handing mine to me first. She turns to each guy, and they soften under her.

"So, Lu, since I haven't introduced my friends. This is Jaspir Ross."

She points at the Viking-styled man who won't stop glaring at me.

"And this is Hawthorn Anderson. But I call him Thorn for short."

"And she can only call me that." Hawthorn narrows his eyes at me

I nod and sip my coffee.

"So where do you work? What's your deal?" Jaspir chimes up

I sit my cup on an end table and cross my right ankle on my left knee.

"I don't work. I inherited a large sum I can live off for a long time. Some may say an eternity."

"hmmm…So you're a rich dude." Jaspir smarts off I smirk at him and chuckle a bit.

"You could say that."

"So then, how do you spend your time?" Elizabeth finally asks

I move my attention from the challenging eyes of Jaspir to Elizabeth's. Her aura is all sunshine and kindness. I hadn't felt such warmth in a long time.

"Well, I read a lot. I enjoy watching the waves. And I have a rescued horse named Noel, I tend to."

I watch as excitement explodes in Elizabeth's emerald eyes.

She clasps her hands together.

"Oh, my goodness! I love horses. May I come to see the horse sometime?"

I clear my throat, taming my excitement down.

"Of course. Noel is big on attention. Well, enough about me. What do you do, Elizabeth?"

"Ellie is okay. That's what my friends call me."

"Okay, Ellie." I smiled with all my charm

Elizabeth's cheeks redden, and she fidgets with her sweater dress. Hawthorn glances at her, and back at me. Once again analyzing me.

"I'm studying art at the college here. Jaspir is on the football team. He wants to go NFL and Thorn is in video game design. He wants to create his own games one day. I want to travel, and paint scenes from wherever I go."

I watched her as she talked about her dreams. The passion was like fire, and it made me smile.

She had such an aura that drew everyone and anything in. Suddenly Hawthorn's watch starts beeping.

"Ellie, we gotta go. Knucklehead must study for this final."

"We can skip it, Hawk. Stay here with E and Lucy."

I grimace at the nickname. Hawthorn takes a glance at my body language and back at Jaspir.

"Do you want to be kicked out of football, Jay?"

Jaspir slaps his knees and stands with a sigh.

"Fine."

Jaspir leans down and kisses Elizabeth's cheek

"Be careful, E" He smirks at me

"Yes, quite careful Ellie." Hawthorn kisses her forehead.

We watch as they leave, and I turn my attention to the window. The sun is setting. Time was flying by with her. That was the first in a long time.

"Wanna get out of here? You said you liked the beach. Would you like to take a walk?"

I meet her eyes, and my heart warms. I nod and stand. I grab her coat before she does, and hold it open for her. She smiles and runs her arms through the black petti coat.

"You are fast and tall." She giggles.

"So, I've been told," I smirk.

I hold my arm out, and she softly intertwines her small arm into mine. We walk to the door and onto the sidewalk.

Chapter Fifteen

The air is cold, and the wind is breezing calm. The sky is clear, and that peace washes over me. I feel Elizabeth shiver.

"Here."

I take my coat off and place her inside of it. It swallows her and hangs past her knees.

"Won't you get cold? I can't take your coat."

I put my hand up to stop her.

"I get warm very easy, and cold not so much."

She eyes me suspiciously but lets it go. I take her arm again, and we make our way to my favorite bench. I sit her down, and then myself.

"So, this is your favorite spot huh?" She looks at me

"Yes. The waves hit the tips of your toes just right. But it always seems to be the calmest near the water. The stars shine a bit brighter above the water."

I feel her staring at me, so I look at her. She's taking me in with such curiosity. A gentle smile is on her face. And her eyes shine just as lovely as the stars above us.

"What? Do I sound silly? Sometimes I do."

"Not at all. Why do you think I paint? Because of what you just described. Beautiful scenes are given to us in nature."

"Is that the only reason you want to travel and paint?"

With that question, she turns to the sky. She wants to avoid my eyes.

"My mother loved to paint. She was amazing. She wanted to go to Paris one day."

"So, your talent is passed down from your mother?"

"Oh yes."

"She must be very proud."

I felt her body stiffen, and the sunshine that poured off her turned cold.

"I wouldn't know. She died a long time ago."

Now my mood was turning cold. I scooted closer to her and placed my hand on her shoulder. I felt her sadness soak my soul. The emptiness.

I felt the real her. The one she covers up with a smile, the bubbly laughs and that sunshine she pours out.

That wasn't her. This was her. A lonely girl who misses her mother, and paints to feel her once again. She gripped my hand and moved it away. She snuggled into my chest, and I held her there.

"I'm sorry, Elizabeth."

I feel a small tremble, and her soul cries out to mine.

"Ellie." She corrects me

"Well, I don't quite like that. Your mother picked a beautiful name."

She raised and stared at me. Her cheeks were wet, and her green eyes were vibrant. I raised my hand and wiped the tears away.

"Who are you? How can I feel like I've known you forever? You are a stranger, but I have no problem not hiding."

I stand and take her hand. She holds onto it and leans into me.

Our bodies feel like we could both burst into flames. I can feel myself wanting to melt into her. But I resisted the urge and just fixed my coat on her.

"I'm not sure what you mean. But sometimes, when you hurt for so long, a stranger is a welcome outlet."

She stares at me for a moment and softly smiles.

"I suppose that could be true. Well, it is getting late." I look at the full moon and sigh.

"Yes. So, it is. I'll walk you home."

"I live at the end of the boardwalk. You don't have to take more time."

"No worries. I gave Noel extra food. He will be fine. Now let's get you home."

She leads me to the end of the shops to a small flat. It's a brick home with a dark roof.

"Well, here I am."

She hands me my coat back. I take it from her and slip it back on. Her scent flies into my nose. Fresh flowers, and a hint of paint swarm inside my senses.

"When can I meet Noel?" She asks unexpectedly

"Anytime. Like I said before I don't do much."

"Well, there aren't any classes tomorrow. I just had a coffee date with Jay and Thorn. Then I'm free. Do you have a phone?"

I pat my jeans pockets and find my iPhone. I hand it over, and she plugs in her number. She hands it back and I look at her contact. She put it under "Ellie, Not Elizabeth.". I smiled and slipped it back into my pocket.

"Okay. Give me a ring, and I'll be there." I nod

"Yes. Goodnight, Lu."

I bend down, lift her face slightly up, and kiss her jawbone.

"Til tomorrow, Elizabeth."

I pulled away to see her face go red. She clumsily unlocks her door. I watch her rush in. She peeks around the door and eyes me. I smirk, turn around, and give her a small wave as I make my way home.

Chapter Sixteen

Elizabeth

After I see him wave, I close the door and lean against it. I felt like my whole body was holding my breath. His presence is like air born heroine. I lug myself behind the door and towards my bed.

I threw my bag on the bed. I walk to my bathroom, run a bath, and light a joint. I watch as the steam swirls up from the water and vanishes. I grab my lavender-scented bubble bath and pour it in.

I throw my clothes off into my hamper and slowly dip myself in.

The warmth envelopes my body, easing away tension and stress. The lavender fills the air, soothing the atmosphere. I inhale on my joint, falling into the calming sensation of the joint and water.

My mind goes back to Lucifer's face. The way he talked about the water and the peace that washed over him. I felt his arms around me as I let myself be vulnerable for the first time in years.

My mother's face flashes back to me, and my heart aches. I hadn't spoken to her in so long. She was the reason I got into painting. I would catch her when dad would be on his bender of being gone, painting away in the backyard on summer days.

She had this waist-length golden blonde hair that fell in waves.

Her eyes were a beautiful crystal blue. When she looked at you, you could feel the warm love just radiating into you. Comfort and security were all I felt when she looked at me. I would run to her, and she would sit me on her lap, and tell me a story of whatever she was painting.

But soon Dad's outings were less, and the painting stopped. He would come home, drunk and angry. Mom wouldn't cook what he liked, or it had too much pepper, then his words would fly.

And if he didn't think those were hurting enough, fists were thrown. One day, my brother and I were watching mom paint. Dad came home unexpectedly and saw her.

My brother and I were terrified. He screamed at Mom. She shielded us, while he broke her easel to pieces. I never saw her cry, even when she took most of the beatings for us.

Not once did she break. Tears ran down my face as the memories hit me in waves. Remembering her was hard. The water started getting cold, so I put my joint out and grabbed my robe. It was late now, and my mind still felt heavy.

So, I picked up my phone off my desk, hit Lucifer's contact, and tucked myself into bed.

"I can't sleep. What are you doing?" I hit send

"I am sitting in my recliner, watching my fireplace. Why can't you sleep?"

I stare at the words and then start to type again.

"I sometimes can't sleep. Well, a lot of the time I can't sleep."

"Why is that?"

I start to tell him why but then erase it and start again. After a few redos, I finally texted back.

"Just stuff, you know. It's one am. I better let you rest. I should be out soon. Thanks for being here, Lu."

"Anytime. Goodnight, Elizabeth." I smile at his reply and respond.

"Not my name, Lu. Goodnight."

I close our chat and turn on my sleep app. I played with the memory of my mother in the sun until my eyes drifted down into sleep.

Chapter Seventeen

Lucifer

I made it home and checked on Noel. He tucked himself in the corner of his barn and fell asleep. I refilled his food and water, softly patted his head, and went inside the cottage.

I started the little fireplace and went to change into pajamas. I had a full-length mirror in the corner of my room. I walked over, took off my shirt, and stared at the scar on my ribs. It was still ridged, and pink. A constant reminder of my betrayal.

The sting of Michael's blade had never gone away. It's stuck with me til eternity. I shake my head and continue to dress. I padded my way to the kitchen and started drinking some tea. Tea had become a comfort. During my time in London, before

Alice turned; we would have a cup during any downtime.

Some habits don't change. I watch as the kettle roars at me. I lift it off the stove and pour it into a mug.

I take a seat on my faithful recliner and stare out my window. I don't own a television. I preferred my own company,

Noel's, or Nature. It was a little past midnight when my phone buzzed. It had been a very long time since it buzzed.

Usually, the only person to buzz me is my home designer asking if I wanted to add to my little heaven.

I sat my mug down and grabbed my phone. The screen lights up, and Elizabeth's contact is displayed.

"I can't sleep. What are you doing?" It reads.

"I am sitting in my recliner, watching my fireplace. Why can't you sleep?"

I watch the little dots go as she types, and my heart flutters.

"I sometimes can't sleep. Well, a lot of the time I can't sleep."

"Why is that?"

The dots pop up and then stop. It goes like that for a while til she finally texts back.

"Just stuff, you know. It's one am. I better let you rest. I should be out soon. Thanks for being here, Lu."

"Anytime. Goodnight, Elizabeth."

"Not my name, Lu. Goodnight."

I smirked down at her reply and lay the phone on the table. I finish my tea, put out my fire, and head to bed. Even the devil needs sleep.

"You won't be able to keep the light, Lucy. You couldn't keep me."

I hear a familiar soft voice with a cutting edge in my ears. I open my eyes. I'm in a cold dark cellar. I'm in my pajama bottoms, without my shirt.

My wrists are chained to the wall. I'm under a small window, that's placed high on the wall. The moonlight streams down onto me. I squint looking all around for the face that belongs to the voice.

"Poor little Lucy. All tied up. Poor little archangel, with no brothers to spare. He takes the souls of those he loves. Bye-bye human, bye-bye human." The voice sings

"Who are you? Where am I?" I ask

I see movement from the corner of the room. The black figure darts to the other corner of the cellar. There is no door to the cellar. It's all four cement walls and that tiny window.

"Who am I? Oh! How could you forget me, Lucky Lucy?" The voice pouted.

My mind whirled. The nickname struck me in the heart. Only one person called me Lucky Lucy. Alice, my lost Alice.

"Alice?"

"Oh, there's my Lucky Lucy. My darling devil."

I watch as she runs to me. She looks the same. She looks like she did before she turned. She looks human.

"Where am I? What have you done?"

"Punishment, Lucy. I've been sent to test you. Well again. Will you lose your light, or save it?" Alice smiled

"What? I have no light. It was taken when I betrayed Father."

This excited her, and she twirled in a circle. Her 1800's dress flowed around her.

"Oh Lucy, see with your eyes." She said widening her own.

She points to another figure in the far-right corner. The shadow is sitting with their knees to their chest, and head resting down. I shake my head and pull against the chains.

My massive ebony wings fly out, and thrash, sending a wave of air at her. She jumps and clasps her hands together.

"Oh, so beautiful. I remember these. Black, black as night. Pretty pretty sight."

She drops to her knees in front of me. She takes her finger and runs it down my abs.

"To save your light, you must reach the darkness. The light is your redemption. But how much will you sacrifice? Will it be true? How far will you go?"

I pulled against my chains, lunging at her.

"I don't understand, Alice."

She jerked her head up, and the demon features were back. The oil ran down her cheeks and the unnaturally wide sharp tooth grin spread across her face.

She goes to the shadow in the corner and grips it by its head. The moonlight hits some of the figure's hair. I see a highlighted deep red bounce off the figure's head.

"Oh, my sweet Lucy, you will. And when you do, you'll know a far greater pain than I was."

And with that, blackness snuffed me out.

I jerked upwards in my bed. My whole body was moist from sweat. My hair was in a tussled mess, and my heart pounded. I ran my hands down my face and held my head in my hands.

My phone buzzed, causing me to jump. Elizabeth's text popped up. I slept til Noon. I grabbed the phone and read her message.

"Hey! I slept in late. I had the weirdest dream. But I just got done with Jay and Thorn. If you're up for it, I'm free."

I texted her back and jumped out of the bed. I quickly threw on some worn blue jeans, a black tee shirt, a purple and black checkered flannel, and my black dress boots. I hurriedly fed Noel and told him I would be right back.

I headed to meet Elizabeth at the Old Brigid, but my mind was still on my dream. I had no idea what it meant. I don't know why I was chained with no escape.

And I have no clue what she meant by saving my light. I had no light. Sure, I had some supernatural strength, speed, flight, and a little bit of magic to change some features. But I had no light. My beauty now held darkness.

The golden angel, the perfect son wasn't there. There was no light to be saved.

Chapter Eighteen

Elizabeth

I barely slept last night after closing my chat with Lucifer. Jaspir and Thorn didn't stay long, so I sat at a small table by a window facing the water. I watched the water crash against the beach.

I was lost in the memory of my dream, my nightmare. I remember being in a dark cold wet place. I was curled up in a corner, terrified. I heard some woman singing, and chains rattling.

All I could see were beautiful ebony wings. But then that woman touched me, and true terror overran me.

It felt like the times my father would grab and hit me. Cold chills ran down my body.

I breathed in and pulled out my sketch pad. I needed to draw those wings. I took out my charcoal pencil and started feathering them out.

I felt somewhat connected to them. I was lost inside my drawing; I didn't notice him come in.

Chapter Nineteen

Lucifer

I made it to the coffee shop. Elizabeth sat inside in the back of the room. She had a sketchbook, and a pencil in hand.

She was sketching something, but I couldn't tell what it was.

I walked in and made it to the table. She looked up from her book startled but smiled and shut it quickly.

"Hello. How are you, Elizabeth?"

"You are very formal, ya know." She chuckled

"So, I've been told. What were you drawing?"

"Oh um….nothing. Let's go. I wanna meet Noel."

She grabbed my hand and dragged me out of the shop.

"Lead the way, captain." She smiled

I didn't rush the walk. This was peaceful, and I craved peace.

I watched the sun highlight the copper in her brown hair, and I wanted to run my hands through it. But even though everything seemed like a dream, something was causing her distraction.

"What?" She spoke, suddenly emerald eyes shined just as much as her hair.

"Is there something the matter? You mentioned a dream in your text."

She pondered over this for a few. We stopped walking, and she stared into the sea.

"It was just a nightmare. Nothing serious."

She investigated the distance. The breeze caught her hair just right and blew it behind her.

"Doesn't seem like nothing."

I watched as she fidgeted with her hands and breathed in deeply.

"It just dug up some feelings I thought I buried. But come on. I want to see Noel. We can talk trauma later." She smiles.

I nodded and lead her up to my cottage.

Chapter Twenty

Elizabeth

His cottage sat back on a cliff from everyone else. It wasn't tiny or big. But that perfect size is in the middle. It was built like a log cabin but cottage style.

It was panels of thick wide wood. There were two small windows in the front. The two faced the town. His roof was made of normal black shingles, but they were rounded at the ends. And a brick chimney puffed smoke.

A few feet from the back of the cottage sat Noel's fenced-in barn. It wasn't as big as a normal barn. But roomy enough for one treasured horse.

I waited at the fence, as he brought Noel out. His home was much more peaceful than my flat.

I watched as he opened the door and led Noel out. He walked him to me, and I gave my hand to him. He sniffed it and then stared at me.

"Hello Mr. Noel, I'm Elizabeth Belle. How do you do?" I smiled

He gave me a few pauses and lowered his head. I patted

his head softly and slow.

"Where did you find him?" I asked Lucifer

"He was just wondering. I found him when he was a baby.

I took him in and nursed him. He was a lost one, but he found a

home."

"Hmmm….We all get a little lost, don't we Noel?"

"But not all of us are found," Lucifer said grimly

We played, fed, and loved Noel until it was time to put

him to sleep. I waited for him to come back out. Up on his cliff,

the stars seemed closer, and brighter. It was quiet here.

The town was so close but here, they seemed so far

away.

"Would you like some tea inside?"

I jumped a little at his sudden approach but agreed. He

led me to his front door and walked me in. Inside was cozy.

He had a small country kitchen; his living room was

medium in size. There was a window above a black loveseat. A

red brick fireplace on the wall faced towards the middle of the

living room.

On the other side of the room was a worn lazy boy and a tall bookcase lined with weathered books.

There was only one painting on the wall. It was of a bright light shining on two people. Their faces were blurred but it was beautiful. The home was humble and beautiful.

"You have a beautiful place here."

I walked to the bookshelf, admiring all the classics.

"I built it myself. I don't do well with too many others, so I built it away from everyone."

"   Doesn't it get lonely? You seem to be here a lot."

I turn from the painting and take a seat on the couch. He's watching the kettle. Sorrow is heavy on his shoulders. I want to run to him. I want to embrace him. Take away the weight I can see him baring.

"Well, that's why I have Noel, my books. They keep me company. The beach is nice as well. The stars are a beautiful sight."

The kettle goes off. I watch as he gathers a tray, and assembles the tea bags, cups, and anything he thinks goes into tea. From milk to honey.

He carefully places it on a coffee table that's in the middle of the loveseat and lazy boy.

I watch as he stirs in a little oat milk, and a squeeze of fresh honey.

I just add sugar and honey to mine. I stir it together leaving my bag but watching him remove his.

"Do you like order?"

He looks up over his cup at me, confused.

"How do you mean?"

"Well, the way you assemble your tea. And the way you outline things."

I watch as a smile appears on his full lips. A real smile, which makes me smile.

"Do you like chaos, and disorder, Elizabeth?"

"You don't like calling me Ellie, do you?" I smirk as I watch him think it over, and that smile remains.

"I like Elizabeth. Nothing else shall do."

He leans forward sitting his cup on the tray. I lower mine down on the tray as well. I close in on him, inches away from his face.

I can feel the raw desire soaking through my bones

"Well, do you mind me calling you Lu?"

He looks up at me. His cyan-blue eyes dig into mine. He takes his index finger under my chin and tilts my face to his.

Our lips are inches from touching. My breathing catches, and my heart pounds. I'm sweating, and my body wants to close the few inches between us.

"Only you, and you alone will ever be allowed to call me that."

His eyes burn into mine, and it feels like centuries pass by as he holds me inches away from his lips. But like that, he drops his finger and sits back in his chair. I'm a bit stunned and try to compose myself.

"Why did you come here? Where are you from? You aren't Scottish. Not with that gruff proper American accent" I change the subject.

I watch as he stands and lights the fireplace, staring into it as he answers me.

"I've been everywhere and nowhere. I don't come from anywhere worth telling."

I stared at him. He's been tense since the day I met him. But when family and his roots are mentioned, he closes completely.

He only replies in sad poem-like words. I stare at my hands as he takes his seat again.

"What about you? Are you from here, or a different part of Scotland?"

Now I'm the one looking into the fire.

"I've always been here. Further on this island than where I live now. We lived outside of town. Only a couple of close neighbors. I was homeschooled by my mother while my brother was a freshman in college."

I can feel him looking at me. I can feel the raw emotions from remembering my family. The emotions I've found are hard not to feel.

"Oh, so you had a close family then?"

I hear real interest in his voice. And it makes me want to share myself with him.

I've never felt like that with anyone. Not even Jaspir and Hawthorn.

"My mother and brother, yes. My father, no."

"Oh. So, no daddy's girl, then?"

He spoke softly. He didn't know how far from the truth that was.

"Not an ounce. He was an abusive drunk. He'd go on these benders. My mother was a painter. A wonderful painter. She was beautiful. Almost angelic. Well, she'd paint, and I'd watch her. My brother too when he was home from classes. She would tell us stories about what she painted. Soon, my father would stay home and get drunk after work. No more bar benders. One day, Mom didn't put her paintings up quickly enough. My brother and I were doing our schoolwork, when dad came busting through the door."

I paused and breathed in. The lump in my throat grew as I told him my trauma.

"My mother hugged us into her arms. We watched as Dad came barreling towards the easel. He smashed her easel to the ground. He broke her pencils, charcoal, and lastly her paints. He grabbed the tubes and squeezed all of them in the trash. He destroyed all of it. She held onto us so tight. But Dad was stronger. For a drunk, you wouldn't think but he was. He ripped her from us and just started hitting her in the face. Screaming how she needs to be doing chores, not painting pretty pictures. I remember trembling in my brother's arms. Just so scared."

I looked at Lucifer as I told him. I knew my eyes were shining with wetness. But he was dark and furious. Not at me, but the wrath of my father.

And that pushed me further to tell him the day my life fell to darkness.

"My mother just took it. But my brother couldn't take it anymore. He broke from me. He pushed our dad away. He held my broken mother. But our dad didn't stop. I never knew he owned a gun. But he had one that day. He stood there pointing a gun at them. I was frozen. My brother laid my mother down and stood in front of her. But my mother was who she was. Our savior. She stumbled up and stood in front of my brother. I still see her face looking at me. She turned to me and spoke her last words. She told me to live and be free. And that's when he was fired. He shot my mother, and as my brother caught her, he shot him in the head next. The next thing I know, my dad comes to me and holds the gun to my temple. But an overwhelming light from somewhere comes out of nowhere. I hear the gun go off, but not on me. On my father. I watch as he falls. He's dead as he hits the ground. I stared at him for a moment but eventually raced to my brother and mother. I don't know how long I screamed. But I screamed and screamed. I felt every bit of pain etched into my very atoms. Eventually, my neighbors took notice and came. I lived out the rest of my childhood in a trusted neighbor's home, and now I'm here."

I stared into the fireplace. I felt tears falling. I finally felt the pain of loss. I felt it in a man's home I barely knew. I fell apart.

Chapter Twenty-One

Lucifer

I raced over to her. She was sobbing. I held her. I felt her breaking in my arms. She held onto the pain for so long. At that moment I was envious of her ability to break because I couldn't break from my pain.

I knew a father's wrath all too well. I knew loss, and I knew what losing a family feels like. But for me, at least I knew they still lived. They did what they had to. She lost her whole family in a span of a few hours. This bond that I feel we've had since the moment our eyes met, made me feel her pain.

Her body shook against me. We stayed like that for a couple of hours until I felt her stop. She became quiet and her breathing was soft. I looked down at her. She had fallen asleep. Cried herself to sleep in my arms.

I slowly drew her into my arms and carried her to my bedroom. I took off her boots and laid them beside the bed.

I covered her with my blankets. I sat softly on the edge of the bed, looking at her. She seemed at peace.

She was truly beautiful. I longed for her. I never had a connection like this to any human.

Something different with this one. She shined, and she sparkled at me. I tucked a piece of hair behind her ear and rose for my pajamas. I headed to my bathroom and changed.

I walked out and saw she was still sleeping. I turned the bedroom light off and went to the living room. The fire was long put out, and the cool draft came into the room.

I bent down and lit the wood again. I stretched and laid myself on the couch. The soft cloth of it warmed my shirtless back. I watched the flames dance as my eyes grew heavy, sleep overtaking me.

Chapter Twenty-Two

I shot upwards. I looked around. I had forgotten I had fallen asleep. I remember telling him about mom and my brother, but then peace.

I fell asleep in his arms, and he must have taken me in here. I rushed to the bathroom, rinsed my mouth with hot water, and toed into the living room.

The sun came shining through his sheer half curtains on the windows. The light hit his chest, causing his fair skin to almost shine.

I walked closer. One arm was slung over his eyes, and the other lay beside him. My eyes traveled down to his abdomen.

My face felt hot as I looked at his six-pack, and that sharp V line peeking up at the top of his checkered pajama bottoms.

"Good morning, Elizabeth."

I almost jumped out of my skin. I thought he was asleep the whole time while I devoured his chest with my eyes.

"Oh. Umm…good morning."

He sat up and ran his hands through his hair. I didn't think anyone could make morning hair and sleepy eyes look so damn sexy, but he did.

I wanted him in that moment so badly

"Did my bed treat you well?"

"Yes. Yes, it was very comfortable."

He smiled at me and stood. He stepped closer to me, and I couldn't move. He towered over me, and I had to look up to face him. I wanted him to take me.

But I felt like something was holding him back. He was holding himself back. I could feel the heat off him. It wanted to burn me with touch. I would have let him burn me, to feel him inside me.

But all he did was grab my hand and softly kiss my knuckles.

Even that gesture made my insides go wild.

"If you excuse me, I need to put something more appropriate on." He smiled

I watched him walk away. His back was just as seductive as his front. I could imagine digging my nails into it. Leaving scars that made him remember I was there.

I snapped my head out of my desires and took a seat on the couch. I turned to the window, staring at the meadows. A part of me never wanted to leave this place.

A part of me wanted to drop out of college, forget my friends, and just stay here. Stay here with him and Noel, in our little blissful heaven.

"Elizabeth, are you alright?"

I hadn't realized he was there. I must have been lost in thought for a few moments.

I took him in. He had put on some bootcut faded blue jeans with a loose gray sweater, and black dress boots.

His black hair was pulled in his normal loose braid. He dressed so much like an English professor.

"Oh, yes. I'm fine. Your meadows look comforting. I guess I got lost in watching them."

"Would you like to have a picnic in them? Unless I'm keeping you from other plans. I know you didn't exactly plan to spend the night"

"I don't have anything to do today. I'd love to."

"We can run you home and grab some clothes, let you shower before we go if you want."

"No that's okay. My mother taught me to be prepared if we ever had to be on the run. Well more if she ever would leave Dad. So, she had gotten me into the habit of storing an extra outfit, and brush in my bag. That's why I carry a deep messenger bag."

"Your mother sounded like a very well-prepared woman."

"Not prepared enough. I'll be right back."

He nodded and I dashed into his bathroom. I threw on a pair of black jogger sweats and a cropped pale-yellow sweater.

I combed my hair into a more uniform ponytail and placed my boots back on.

I stepped back into the living room, but he wasn't there. I opened the front door and saw him tending to Noel.

I waited for him near the small gate of his stable.

Chapter Twenty-Three

Lucifer

"Hello, Mr. Noel. You be good today. Elizabeth and I are going to picnic in the meadows. What do you think of her?"

I patted his snout as he did his usual approval neigh. I smiled and led him to his bed. I placed his food and water and took my leave. I saw Elizabeth waiting for me and jogged to her.

I had already packed our food and drinks while she was dressing. The perks of being a higher being.

"Are you ready?" I asked

She looked at the basket, confused.

"Wait, how did you make that up so fast?"

"Oh, I'm pretty fast you know." I smiled

She nodded, and we headed to the meadows a few miles from the back of the cottage.

The wind was warm today, and the sun shined brightly. Spring was on its way. We found a nice spot and laid out the blanket and food.

"You know, you haven't mentioned your family very much or anyone at all."

I made our tea and handed her the cup. I stared at the swaying flowers and considered her statement. I wasn't open with anyone anymore. I instantly wanted to guard myself.

"Lu, it's okay if it's hard to speak on. I hadn't spoken really about the day they died to anyone. Sometimes being able to break, to feel whatever emotions they bring is good. It makes you feel less heavy."

I stared at her. She was so real, so alive. She was full of life. I was full of dying embers. I wanted to feel her raging fire inside me.

Maybe hoping it would spark my own back to life. Her emerald eyes soothed me and calmed me.

"My family and I no longer speak. I have no mother. My brothers and father banished me. I'm alone. I had some friends who came with me and supported me against my family's wrath. But soon, they too left me. Some have died, and others lay low."

Elizabeth rolls the information in her head.

"Are you some kind of crime boss?" She asks

I pause and look at her. She's serious, and that makes me laugh. She is taken aback but a toothy grin spreads across her face.

"What? No. I'm just well I'm just me. Alone." I shallowly smile.

"I'm here. Noel is here. So, you aren't alone. Not anymore anyhow."

"Yes, I suppose that is true." I smirk

"So, what made you come here? I know you aren't from here."

I wish I could tell her I'm from above, but I can't, and it doesn't matter since I'm no longer allowed through the gates.

"I moved around a lot. I don't remember much of my younger years. But I lived in America. Ohio to be specific. Then London for a few years, and now I'm here."

Elizabeth nods and takes a bite of a chocolate muffin.

I turn my attention to the sky. It's the clearest it's been for a while. It's beautiful. Elizabeth stood and lay beside me.

"This meadow and this sky, my mother would have loved to have painted."

I turn my head towards her. Our faces are so close. She turns her head, and we stare into each other's eyes.

"Lu, what aren't you telling me?"

The sudden question makes me pause for a moment.

"How do you mean?"

"You feel guarded. And don't ask how I feel it, but I do. You can trust me."

"I know."

I prop myself on my elbow and stare down at her. She's stunning. Her freckles are placed perfectly across the bridge of her nose. I reach my hand and stroke her cheek. Her skin is pale and smooth. I bend down, cup the side of her face, and press our lips together.

I feel a shock shot through my body. Something feels awakened in me. I feel that spark hitting my dying embers. Her soft lips kiss back with need. I roll over onto her. I grab the back of her head and kiss her more frantic. My hands want to rip her clothes off and dig my fingers into her tight vagina. But I resist the urge and force myself to release her. I sit up panting.

Chapter Twenty-Four

Elizabeth

I've been kissed before but never felt like I did when he kissed me. Every cell in my body felt charged. I felt like I could fly. I felt connected to him. The bond I had sensed felt even stronger now.

But the desire for him to slam himself into me was just as intense. I wanted him to use his fingers and fuck me til I came. I wanted him to insert himself so deep inside me, I could feel it in my guts. I wanted to be used so through that he'd have to carry me home.

I watched as he dragged his hands through his hair. I could feel his chaos brewing.

"Lucifer, are you alright?"

I heard him sigh and watched as he gathered up the picnic.

"Um, yes. I am fine. I just lost control for a moment." I placed my hand on his forearm and stared into his eyes.

"You didn't do anything wrong, Lu."

"You don't understand. I can't do that with you. I can't hurt you."

I was confused. He was shaken up, and worried. I grabbed his arms, making him stop gathering the items. I held his hands to my chest.

"You won't hurt me. See, my heart is still beating."

"No. I won't allow last time to repeat itself."

"What? What do you mean?"

"It's nothing."

"Tell me, Lu. What's wrong?" I asked, my tone sharp.

And that's when I felt the air around him shift. It felt heavy and dark. He got on top of me, and pressed my back to the ground, pinning my arms down. He was inches from my face. His cyan eyes were now navy blue.

"I can't fuck you, Elizabeth. I can't. But I want to so badly. I want to stroke your lips with my fingers. I want to lick your cum as it drains from you. I want to bury my cock so far inside you that even when it's not there you will still feel it. I want to claim your body inside and out."

My breath hitched as he traced his lips down the curve of my neck. His hot breath warmed my skin.

"You can have me, Lu. Please take me." I whispered.

"I can't."

He rose from me, finished cleaning up the picnic, and reached his hand to me.

"I'll walk you home."

The walk home was quiet. Our kiss changed something in him. He kept me at a distance. He was shielding me from himself.

We arrived at my flat. I put the key in and turned it over. I turned around to say goodbye, but he wasn't there.

My heart dropped and I felt like I was losing him. I barely knew him. But something just clicked with us.

It's as if we were always meant to find one another. Like pieces of a puzzle, we just fit. I walked into my flat, laid my things on my desk, and sat in front of my easel.

College won't be back until next year. We were meant to take this time and use our skills for internships, but I had no desire. Hawthorn went away til college started again to see family.

Jaspir decided to move to a different college in America of all places.

So yes, I was truly alone. So, I did what I do best. I sat on my easel and chose to do some kind of charcoal picture. I stared at the blank canvas. I didn't know what to make.

Suddenly my head started pounding. It felt as if something wanted to take over. The pain proceeded to get worse.

A stabbing searing pain over and over. I couldn't take it anymore and let whatever it was take me over. I felt this dark cloud inside me. I felt dirty and unclean.

I watched as my hand took off drawing with the charcoal. Swift sweeps of feathers appeared on the canvas. They were big and thick ebony color. Then I watched as my hand started a body in the middle.

He was on his knees. his hands were shackled, and long chains that were attached to the shackles hung from a concert wall. He was shirtless, he was well-toned, and his head was bent. Black long hair hung over his face, and tears were dropping to the floor.

The person felt familiar. But I couldn't tell who it was. The hair covered his face.

My hand finished the male and moved on. Next, I watched as I drew a woman with tight black curls, who wore an old dress. But she held someone in her arms. This girl was lying in her arms.

Her eyes were closed, and she wore a normal white tee shirt and jeans. But the shirt wasn't colored except in one spot. It looked like the girl was wounded, a fatal wound.

Below the girl were large feathers. They were tattered and spotted. I moved my eyes to the woman holding the girl. And I was suddenly overwhelmed with fear. Her pupils weren't normal. They were shaped like a thick forked road and black.

The darkest black ran down her cheeks, and a toothy grin spread unnaturally across her face.

Her teeth were sharp. My heart raced with fear. It felt as if she was staring at me, into me.

"Watch out pretty, watch out."

I jumped at the voice, and whatever took over me was gone. I had control again and the pain was over. My breathing quickened and I shivered. I looked at my picture, finally taking in the scene.

The man was an angel, a sad angel. He was beautiful. But I had no clue if the girl was one too. She had feathers beneath her, but I just couldn't gather. The woman, she was evil. I could feel it. This felt like a dream I had a few days ago. But it was more detailed on this canvas.

I shook my head and ran my hands down my face. I paced back and forth. I felt like I was being watched once whatever just entered me left.

I felt trapped inside of my flat. So, I grabbed my coat and walked out. I needed to get out, to clear my mind.

I breathed in the chilled air and started my way to the beach.

Chapter Twenty-Five

I made it home, took care of Noel, and placed myself in my armchair. I felt bad for flying away from Elizabeth, but I was losing control. I could feel it slipping away.

My desire to make her mine was too much. I knew what taking her would turn her into, and she was too pure. Her shine couldn't be demolished, at least not by me.

I pulled out my phone and stared at our last messages. I wanted to call and tell her I was sorry for taking off but maybe if she felt like I was an ass, she could save herself from me. All I've done was bring pain and death. In heaven and on earth, all I have done is hurt those I love.

I wouldn't do that to her, I just couldn't. I put the phone down and went to my room. I turned off the bedroom light and just lay in bed. I had no energy to change. The dark was comforting when my mind and heart would fight.

They say that we all of an angel and devil on our shoulders, but it is just our hearts and minds at war with one another.

I felt like I had run a marathon trying to control my urges that I had finally given up, and let my eyes fall. I don't know how long I had fallen asleep, but I awoke suddenly.

My whole body was vibrating with alarm. Something was wrong, I felt my heart weighing with panic. I couldn't place it.

I turned over and grabbed my phone. My gut was screaming at me for Elizabeth. But Elizabeth should have been home. She didn't seem the type to welcome danger.

I dialed her number anyway, but no pickup. I kept dialing it. It was about four in the morning. Elizabeth would be up.

She told me she wasn't good at sleeping. My heart pounded with stress. I couldn't go to sleep. I slipped on my boots and made my way to her flat.

Chapter Twenty-Six

<u>*Elizabeth*</u>

I made it to the beach and sat on the sand. I watched the soft waves tickle my bare toes. This place, besides Lu's cottage, was very peaceful. I felt a sense of ease staring at the water. The air was quiet, and the stars were bright.

I had a random small sketch pad and pencil in my pocket. It was the size of one of those twenty-page memo pads. Mom had done it, and I took the idea with me. I have one in each coat, even if I have my messenger bag with my normal pad.

I opened the pad and started to draw the sky reflecting in the water. I was sketching away when goosebumps rose on my arms. A surge of bitter taste coated my tongue and dread covered me. I stopped sketching, stood up, and looked around me. I didn't see anyone.

The town slept. I was about to sit down and shrug it off until I heard a voice.

"Hello pretty. I see you. I see who you really are."

I turned my eyes to where the voice spoke out. It was coming from behind a tree, right where the sand stops. My mind was telling me to run, to get away. But I couldn't.

I needed to know who this was. This person felt like the cloud that took me over.

I started walking towards it.

"What do you mean? I'm me. I'm no one."

I heard the voice laugh, and I got closer.

"You are more than you know. Come closer."

I stepped closer, and as I did, a clawed hand flew around the tree and ripped into my shoulder. I felt a burning pain flooding my body.

The blood was warm and soaking through my sweater.

I watched as the figure moved from the tree and over me.

It was the woman from my dream and picture. My eyes grew wide, and fear gripped me. She was scarier in person. She raised her hand and tore into my thigh.

I screamed in agony. Her eyes grew wide, and that grin looked at me. She sucked my blood from her fingers.

"I knew it. But I won't kill you just yet. I'll hurt you real bad. That will get to him. Maybe if he can see how weak you are, how much human you are more than the other, he will forget you. He will reign with me."

I stared at her in confusion. My body felt as if I was on fire. I couldn't understand what she meant.

"What? I'm all human. I don't know what you mean."

She crouched down and put her face inches from mine.

I could smell the decay coming off her, and the evil wanting to sink into me.

"You aren't all human. There is some grace in there. I tasted it in your blood. You are more than a human, girl. But you are weak. That side of you isn't strong. I'm guessing that little bit of grace came from Mommy didn't it?"

"What?"

"I can sense it. This belonged to Mommy. Daddy was the human. Tell me, did mommy feel like the sun?"

I couldn't comprehend what she was telling me. I always saw my mother as a pure figure. She always felt good.

"She was my mother. Of course, she felt like the sun. She was my comfort and my peace. She was a light in the darkness."

I felt tears overflowing down my cheeks. My body was in pain and my mother's memory added to it.

"See, I can see the light in you. It's bright. And he's attracted to it. He thinks it will absolve him from all he's done. But my Lucky Lucy, has done no wrong. But that stupid light of yours, the little bit of grace your mother somehow made bright, makes him love you. Well, I'll take your light, that tiny bit of grace. Not today, no. I'm leaving you broken here. But soon, oh so soon, I will kill you. That redemption he thinks you'll bring will be gone. Then he will have me beside him as we burn this earth, as we turn these weak humans into demons. We will feed on humanity and we will be their God."

"Who are you talking about? I don't know what you are or what you mean by I have grace. But you are wrong."

She stood and danced around me. She twirled like those girls in ball gowns around me.

"Lucky Lucy is Lucifer, pretty. And you, my dear, are his love. That light of yours is his redemption."

My eyes widen, and my mind is sent spiraling. Lucifer is who she is speaking of. My picture comes flashing into my mind. He's the angel in it. The pull I feel for him starts to make sense to me now.

"Is that why he's so cautious of letting me in?"

This makes her stop dancing. Her grin spreads from ear to ear and she cuts her eyes into mine.

"He lets you in, you become like me. Or at least that's what he thinks will happen. The thing is that Lucky Lucy doesn't understand the light he sees. He doesn't know that the light is grace. He doesn't know that once he connects to you in that way, some of his darkness will fall away. He won't return to heaven, but he will regain some of his strength. But it will be too late once he knows this."

"The picture you drew with my hands," I whisper

This makes her happy. She claps and jumps up and down like a kid getting a gift.

"Oh yes. You'll die with him watching. Once you are gone, his hope will be demolished, and his real self will be out. The true

morning star will bring hell on earth."

The man she speaks of isn't the one I've come to love in such a short period. He doesn't want to do those horrible things. He wants to find peace, and someone to love him.

"He's not that man you speak of. He's the calm in the storm. He's remorseful. He misses his family. He's good." She laughs loudly.

"Silly girl. He's not any of that. He's a bloodthirsty king. And he will rule, and I'll be his right hand, his lover. Now enough of this."

She opens her mouth, letting out a piercing high-pitched tone that makes my ears bleed, and then I watch as her foot comes crashing into my face. My vision blacks and I hear her skipping away singing.

Chapter Twenty-Seven

Lucifer

I arrived at her flat. I knocked but no one answered.

"Elizabeth, open up. It's Lucifer."

I waited, and still no response. I thought maybe she had ended up smoking and falling into a heavy sleep. But I had to make sure.

My gut still felt tied in a knot. I waved my hand at the deadbolt and heard it click over. All the lights were off, and it was silent.

I walked further into the room, going towards her bed. It was empty, and so was the bathroom. Her flat was empty.

She wasn't with her friends because Jaspir no longer lived there, and Hawthorn was away. I continued to look for signs of where she may have gone when her easel caught my attention.

I switched on her light and took in the picture. My mouth dropped. I had this picture play out in my dream. I didn't know how Elizabeth would know about it. I never told her.

She had mentioned her strange dream before but didn't go on about it.

I stood staring at the picture when a tingling sensation ran down my spine. A sudden fear pierced my heart.

"Lu…Lucifer."

It was Elizabeth's voice. It was far away, and weak. Even so, I knew where she was now. Her light called to me. It was weakening, she was weakening. Something happened to her, and it wasn't just a coffee run.

I closed her door and took off to the beach. When I made it, I saw Elizabeth lying on the grass. Her right hand was holding onto the left inner of her thigh, and her left hand held onto her right shoulder. She was bloodied. Her nose was swollen, and her right eye was black. Her lip was busted.

A rage burned in me. I touched her pulse. It was weak but she was alive.

"Oh, Elizabeth."

I lifted her gently in my arms. She let out a sharp cry and collapsed into me. I wasted no time, so I flew her to my cottage.

Noel neighed at me with worry as we approached.

"I won't let her go, boy. It will be alright."

He huffed and trotted back into his bed. I walked through the door and placed her on my bed. Her sweat was ripped, and so were her sweater, and coat. All of it bloody.

I slowly took her pants off and cut her shirt off. The wounds were deep. But they had stopped bleeding. I was confused at that because these wounds were so deep.

A human wouldn't be able to withstand it, let alone be able to stop bleeding at this level.

I grabbed a wet rag and softly patted her wounds.

"Lu... What's happened?"

Elizabeth stared at me. Tears welled up, and it made her green eyes shine.

"I found you. You were wounded, and bloody."

She laid back, and small tremors ran through her body.

"I don't know who she was."

"She?"

"Not right now. I... need sle-"

She passed out once again. I sighed and grabbed the first aid kit. I wrapped her wounds and covered her up. I went to stand up, but she grabbed my hand. She didn't open her eyes.

"Don't go. Stay, please."

She was half asleep. I kissed her hand.

"Okay."

I tucked her back in and changed into my pjs. I shut the lights off and lay next to her. She moved closer to me, and I pulled her into a tight hug. Something attacked her. A "she" Elizabeth recalled. She was too worn and scared.

I listened to her breathing, softly drifting to sleep myself.

Chapter Twenty-Eight

Elizabeth

I wasn't with Lucifer. I didn't feel his arms around me, but I did feel the sun. I was walking in his meadow. It was warm, and the sun was shining on my skin.

"Bethy, come here."

I recognized that voice. It was my mother. She appeared a few feet in front of me. She was dressed in a long white dress again. Her long blonde hair rested on her back to her waist. She was painting on her worn easel.

I approached her, and she looked the same. She had the same piercing green eyes.

The same deep dimples. The same comfort and warmth glowed from around her. She took my hand and held it to her chest.

"Mom? But how?"

"We don't have much time. I am so sorry about your earlier life honey. I am sorry about Matthew. I know he died too. But he's okay. He's happy. I am here because you lived. You lived for a reason. I should have told you when I was still here. But you aren't completely human. You have some of my grace in you. That's why you were spared. I'm not human. I am, I was an angel. A fallen angel. I lost a little over half of my grace. Once I became pregnant with you, it went down even more and into you."

I stood shocked. My mind kept telling me that this was only a dream. But my heart knew just like the one I drew at home that it all was real.

"What about Matt? He was the firstborn." I press.

"I'm not sure why it skipped him. But it did. Now, I need you to listen carefully. I know what you've been up to. I think that's why it passed to you. You can give the devil a home. Your light can give him peace."

"What?" My mind whirled

"Lucifer. I fell with him. I was among the loyalists. I met your father; over the years, he became what he did—no influence from my grace. Listen to me, you can save him. Forget what the churches told you, forget what they preach on Sundays. You've met him and you've fallen in love with him. You know what his soul bears. We know that Alice is trying to turn him."

"Alice?"

"You've met her. She was his first love. She lost her humanity once they made love. It's corrupted her. She's gathered others with her. She plans to make him hopeless so that he will have nothing. He will have nothing to fight for. She wants to bring hell on earth."

"It was her who hurt me. But how am I supposed to save him? All I am is some bright light everyone says can see but me. I don't have wings, super strength, or telepathy. All I can do is paint.
She found me and hurt me. I can't do anything."

Mom pulled me closer to her and pointed at the canvas in front of her.

"Look."

I turned and saw the painting that Lucifer had in his cottage.

The bright light with figures praising it.

"What is this?" I asked

"This is what is to pass. When it's time to fight, you will know. It will be instinct that takes over and saves him, and earth."

I stared at the painting more.

"But my dream had him in chains. Alice held me, and I was wounded or dead."

"When love is involved, sacrifice is the only salvation. Now I must go. They limited my time."

"Wait! Who's they?"

"Home. We want to see him happy too. Don't believe what man preaches. We stand for love and forgiveness. His soul cries for forgiveness. And you, my beautiful daughter was made to give him that."

"But how are you in heaven? Where will he go?"

"Because of you. I was granted to be with your brother because you will be the one to save all of the earth and give redemption to the greatest evil. As for Lucifer, he will live forever, even after you are gone."

"We aren't related, right? I mean you are an angel. They say we are all family."

My mother chuckled.

"No. We don't believe in brother-sister here. We are just here. We are just another creation before God's favorite creation was made. We are just beings. But Lucifer's home was with us. He and the other archangels have always been close. But maybe with Lucifer being among the humans for so long, he has started thinking of all of us like family."

I nodded and stared into her face.

"I miss you." Tears ran down my face

"I know. And I miss you. One day we will be together, but not soon. Years to come. Now get back to him. Save him. We will be watching."

She slipped her hands from mine, and I watched as she walked away.

"Bye, sister!"

I saw a glimpse of Matthew, as he waved at me and then took Mom's hand. They faded away and I'm shocked out of my sleep. "Mom." I gasp

I watch as Lucifer sits up too. He stares at me like I might break right there.

"Elizabeth, what's wrong?"

I stare up at him and see him for who he truly is. I can see the mask is gone. The blue eyes are now the dying embers of a fire.

I can see the air around where his second face once was. I can see his brute strength cut down to half mass. I can see the sadness from missing home. I can see his four massive ebony wings folded against his back. I see Michael sending him to earth with a mighty spear. I can see his soul. The darkness fogged up the light trying to break through.

I reach my hand out and place it on his cheek. He leans into it.

"I see you. I see you, Lu."

Chapter Twenty-Nine

I looked at her face and noticed her wounds had healed to very light bruising.

"Yes. Your eyes do look better. I don't know how you are healing this fast. Humans usually take much longer."

She reached her hand out to stop me and placed it on her chest.

"What? Is something else hurting you?" I watched as a small smile crept across her face.

"I had a dream. It had your meadow, but Mom was there. And my brother."

"That sounds lovely, Elizabeth."

"But here is the thing. She was more than I knew, and I'm more than I knew."

I'm staring at her, confused. She scoots in closer to me.

"In my dream, my mother told me she was a part of your loyalist angels. When she fell, she lost almost all of her grace. For some reason, Matty didn't get any of it, but when she had me, it got passed down to me. I'm not completely human. I mean I am more human than an angel. I only have a tiny bit."

I have no words to tell her. Dreams are dreams. But these dreams lately have been shared. Her wounds healing so quickly but not completely flood my mind. Her dream could explain that.

Of all the souls to fall in love with, it's one with a little grace.

"That would explain why you healed to scars and light bruising then. What does all this mean? How did your mother know? Why didn't she find me?"

Before she could respond, my front door busted open, throwing it into the end of the kitchen island.

I pushed Elizabeth further up the bed and leaped off it softly to investigate. I saw her yellow dress spinning and her voice singing echoed in my ears.

"Lucky Lucy, where art thou?"

"Alice."

She spun around and that grin of hers spread.

"Awe, there he is. Where is she, Lucy?"

"Where is who?"

"The barley angel. Give me that mistake so we can rule."

I closed my bedroom door and stood in front of it. I crossed my arms over my chest, and my four ebony wings emerged behind me. Alice's black eyes widened, and her hands flew to her mouth in awe.

"Oh, I forgot how beautiful those are, Lucy."

"You won't have her."

She moved her stare from my wings to mine and cocked her head.

Almost like a dog would at a strange noise. I hated it so much.

My old Alice was intelligent, human. Now she's empty, all void inside. She skipped to me and ran her fingertips along my biceps.

"Now Lucy, don't make me bring my friends in. We all know the great and powerful serpent of the garden isn't all that mighty anymore."

I stood my ground and didn't move an inch.

"If I'm not mighty anymore, why kill her and have me rule this world?"

She danced away, into the middle of the living room.

"The one thing that has always stopped you from truly being powerful Lucy is love. Once it's gone, you'll be who you have always been. The perfect being, the wisest and the most strong."

Before I could respond, two men walked through the door. They were tall like me and built like linebackers. Spread behind them were dirty and tattered wings.

"Hello, King." They spoke.

They were twins. Both looked the same. I knew them right away. They were the first to follow me in heaven.

"Leon and Luther? I thought you had died. How is this possible?"

"Me. I gave them life. Now I will give you life Lucy." Alice smiled

"You won't have her."

Alice shrugged her shoulders and whistled. Leon and Luther took off at me. They grabbed each arm, threw me at the wall next to the door, and held me there. I pressed against them, but they had such brute strength I couldn't move them.

"What did she do to you?"

"She gave us extra power. Her blood is magic." Luther smiled "You dirtied yourself with that tainted blood?"

"What have you had us done? You left us. You left us all. To what? To dance in the flowers? To raise a horse? To love human filth? You abandoned us, and she found us." Leon spoke with anger.

I felt his anger fuming off of him. They died in the fall. My twin warriors died when they landed. I laid them out in a place I thought no one could find them so they would have peace, but Alice found them.

She woke their rest with demon blood. She made their grace sour into hell oil.

"I am so sorry. I didn't know I could bring you back."

"Enough. Hold him there."

Alice walked towards the bedroom door and knocked. I fought against their hold, but I couldn't break it.

"Little Lizzy, please be dressed. You have guests."

She walked through the doors, and Elizabeth started screaming but then abruptly stopped. I pressed harder against them.

But they wouldn't budge. I was weak. Alice dragged Elizabeth out with her hair. She had knocked her out.

"We won't kill her here. I have a place."

Chapter Thirty

Elizabeth

I woke up to the sound of chains rattling. I was cold and was lying on hard ground. When I opened my eyes, I thought I was dreaming.

The dream I had drawn was right in front of my eyes. But now I knew who I dreamt about. Lucifer. My Lucifer. He was in the same chains. He was shirtless in his sleeping pants. And his beautiful ebony wings were spread behind him.

His head was bowed, and he was pale. I rose from the ground and started walking towards him, but I was yanked back.

"Not yet, little Lizzy. Not yet."

Alice's sing-song voice stung my ears.

I struggled against her, but it was no use. On the outside of the cell were two angels. Since I dreamed of Mom, it had awakened something in me. I could see auras now.

I could tell what beings they are and if they are good. Those angels were a steel gray. They didn't have good or bad coming off them. They were just there. I looked at Alice, and all I saw was emptiness. Her aura was the deepest black, and evil just flew all around her.

I turned my attention to Lucifer, and I was taken aback. A soft warm golden glow surrounded him. It was like the time of the day when the sun was setting, and it was coming through a window.

It wasn't a blinding light; it was a warm inviting light. It was a comforting light off of a night light. He exploded with remorse and goodness.

Alice dragged me over and made me get on my knees in front of Lucifer. He raised his head and our eyes met. His true eyes were there.

He didn't hide them with the cyan blue I had come to know. This time he let the dying embers be seen. It was like the last few flames of a fire that was almost out. But not quite out yet. There is just a touch of fire left with the ash.

"Your eyes are beautiful."

"Shut up." Alice lashed out

Her hand smacked me in the cheek, and I whimpered out. I grabbed my cheek and held it.

Lucifer growled and tugged against his chains. My heart ached for him. Those chains were cutting into his wrists. I wanted to take them off. But I wasn't strong enough. I was only a human with a little grace.

"Growl as you wish. Soon you'll be screaming, then you will rule."

"I'll die before you lay another hand on her."

Alice giggled and bent down beside me.

"You know how this goes, Lucy. You both had the dream and you, little Lizzy, not only had the dream but also drew it. So, you know how it goes. But I want to have some fun, okay."

She grabbed my arm and threw me at the wall. My body impacted it with a vibrating thump. My body felt like it had been hit by a truck.

I slid down the wall, holding onto my arm. I felt it snap when it hit the wall.

"Oh, did I break your arm? Poor human."

"STOP! PLEASE, ALICE." Lucifer yelled

But it only made her happier. She drew her foot up and kicked me on the left side of my face. It sent me face-first onto the cold concrete of the cell.

My breathing quickened and I felt so broken. My face was swelling, my right arm was broken above the elbow to my wrist. Alice gripped my hair and dragged me to Lucifer. She put me on my knees.

I tasted the blood running from my nose into my mouth. His eyes burned, and tears ran down his cheeks. I reached my hand out and stroked his cheek. I smiled at him.

I couldn't speak. I was in too much pain. Suddenly his face went from pain to gutted horror. I couldn't hear him, but I knew he was screaming in agony.

I could feel his aura turning from the warm sunset to burning lava. Then that's when I felt the sharp blade.

I looked down at my stomach to see Alice had stabbed a small sword through it. My eyes filled with tears. My hand fell from Lucifer's face, and I slumped to the ground.

Chapter Thirty-One

Lucifer

"ELIZABETH! ELIZABETH! NO!!!!" I screamed

My vision went red. All I can see is the sword ripping through her stomach, and the blood pooling underneath her.

She was right there, touching me, reassuring me, loving me, and the next she was dying on the ground. My Elizabeth, dying.

"Miss. Alice, what's next?" Leon asks.

Alice jumps and claps. She races over to the brothers and in one swift motion, she cuts their throats. I tremble with anger.

Elizabeth is dying because of her, and now my dear friends who were misguided have been killed. Alice skips to me and bends down to my eye level. That grin is full of happiness.

"Now Lucy, since they are out of the way, and Elizabeth will be soon as well, we can embark on the next task. You will take up what your heavenly host labeled you, and damn every human soul possible. I'll be your queen."

I drop my head, and tears spill even more from my eyes. My heart is breaking in two, and my anger is at boiling level.

"Doesn't that sound nice, Lucky Lucy?"

She touches my shoulders.

A surge of power I haven't felt since I fell, hits throughout my body. It feels like Zeus has sent a lightning bolt coursing through my veins.

I rip the chains off the wall, setting myself free. I stand and hover over Alice. She shrinks before me and backs away into the far-right corner of the cell.

I follow and lift her by the throat.

"I will not be ruling or damning any souls. You will not be my Queen. You are not the woman I had loved. You are the shell of the Alice I knew. You are lost, Alice. You've lost the one thing that makes us imperfect beings, perfect. The capability to love."

"No, Lucy. She's your weakness. Yup, yup. Weak. Once she's dead, we will be Gods."

"No Alice. I don't want to be a God. I never should have wanted that. I have regretted that since the day I lost my home."

"No. No. No. Not true. Mmmm not true."

I watched her slowly lose it even more. The Alice I had loved was gone completely. I had finally broken her. I couldn't save her, and so I did what was left to do. I broke her neck and laid her down. I raced over to Elizabeth.

The small sword was still protruding from her stomach. She was pale, and her breathing was weak.

I placed her on my lap, and rocked her gently, kissing her forehead.

"Don't go. Please don't go." I cried

"I'm so tired."

"No. Don't go to sleep. You won't wake up. I need you." She reached her hand to my face and pulled me to hers.

"I felt your power come back. They said if I saved you, you'd be okay. Maybe that's what they meant. I felt you burn like an erupting volcano. Your power is back. I felt it."

"I don't care about that. I don't care about being full of power or barely any at all. I care about you. I care about you."

Tears dropped on her cheeks, and she smiled up at me. She felt lighter. She felt peaceful.

"I love you, Lu."

Her hand dropped from my face and hit the ground beside her.

Her body stopped trembling.

"No. You can't go. FATHER, YOU BRING HER BACK! TAKE MY STUPID POWER, TAKE THESE WINGS. JUST BRING HER BACK! I CAN'T DO THIS! YOU CAN'T TAKE MY LIGHT. YOU CAN'T HAVE HER FATHER, YOU CAN'T HAVE HER!" I screamed

I couldn't move. I held her there. I placed my forehead to hers and rocked us back and forth.

Chapter Thirty-Two

Elizabeth

The air felt warm, and the sun shined on my skin. I opened my eyes to see I was lying in a field of bright pink and yellow tulips.

"I've been waiting."

Sitting beside me was Mom. Her long golden blonde hair was flowing behind her. She had her knees to her chest, and she was staring off into the field. I heard a child's laughter and sat up.

Matty was playing in the field with other adults. He was small again, and happy.

"Am I in heaven? I died?"

She turned and smiled at me.

"My version of heaven. But it's not your time yet. I just needed to talk before you go back."

"How? I was stabbed in the gut. There's no turning back."

"There is if a higher power says that's the plan."

"What?"

"Bethy, you saved him. He's willing to give up his wings, his power, his life to bring you back. The greatest evil, the most prideful being in all creation, the most perfect son wanting to give up the one thing he ever loved for a mortal with a touch of grace? I'd say that's the biggest save in creation."

"What happens next then? Will he lose everything if I'm back?"

Mom turns to me and takes my hand.

"Nothing. You will be with him until it's your time. That's when I'll see you again."

"But what will happen to him?"

"Bethy, only the big guy knows. But I have a feeling some loopholes will happen. Now it's time to go back. I will see you again. I love you."

As mom kissed my forehead, I'm shot out of the field, and back into Lucifer's arms.

Chapter Thirty-Three

Lucifer

"You can't have her, father. You can't."

"Lu…"

I look down at Elizabeth in shock. I look her over. The sword is gone, and all she has left is some faint bruising. I lift her shirt up and on her stomach is a scar. I'm shaking with happiness.

"Elizabeth, oh Elizabeth."

I press my lips against hers. She kisses back with the same feverish desire. I pulled back and examined her face.

"What happened? How did you come back? The sword is gone. Your wounds are healed."

She smiled at me and wrapped her arms around my neck.

"It wasn't my time according to a higher power." She whispered in my ear.

I lifted her in my arms and looked over at Alice's lifeless body.

"It's not your fault, Lu. She couldn't have been saved. She lost her mind."

"Yes. But she and my fellow angels were killed. I hate all the killing, the bloodshed. I hate all the darkness."

Elizabeth cups my face and makes me look at her. Her emerald eyes radiate love at me, and it makes my heart race.

"Let's go home, Lu. Take me home." I nod and fly off with her in my arms.

We make it back to the cottage, and Noel comes trotting with anger in his hooves at us.

"I'm sorry, Noel. So much has happened. I'm so happy you are okay."

I pet his snout and kiss it.

"Let me put Elizabeth to rest, and I'll be back.

"No, it's okay. I can walk. Take care of him."

I place her gently on her feet and watch as she walks into the cottage.

"Okay boy, let's get you settled."

I feed and water him. I make his bed up and kiss him goodnight.

I walk into the living room and see Elizabeth cleaning up the broken door. I rush over and take it from her.

"Hey. I'm trying to help here." She huffs at me.

"Let me."

I take the front door, lean it against the broken hinges, and snap my fingers. Just like that, it's fixed. Being at full power feels new again.

It had been so long since I've been max power. It almost feels foreign in my veins. Elizabeth smirks and sits down on the couch. She lit the fireplace while I was outside.

I sit beside her, taking her hands into my own. "What's on your mind, Elizabeth?" She looks at me and smiles.

"Since I've met you, I've felt full. We were made for one another, literally. I don't want to go back to school. I want to be with you. I want to travel with you. I want to paint in every place we go. I just want to live. Live til my time is up, and I can see Mom and Matty."

"Oh course! We can do that. Paris first, right?" I grin

"Are you sure? You know if you get attached to me, it'll hurt like a bitch once I die."

I laugh and take her into my lap. I lift her chin with my pointer finger.

"I'll feel you, nonetheless. Little pieces of you will always be with me and around me. You won't die completely."

"I love you, Lucifer."

"I love you, Elizabeth. You are perfectly made."

"Even if I'm only a human with a touch of grace?"

"Perfectly made, Elizabeth. My human with a touch of grace."

I kiss her

In the depths of darkness, I found a love that could conquer even my fiercest evils. I found my light.

And in the beginning, I was lost but at the end of our love story, I was found.